The Ghost of Genny Castle

by

John Escott

Illustrations by Dilys Jones

Cassell · London

CASSELL LTD.
35 Red Lion Square, London WC1R 4SG
and at Sydney, Auckland, Toronto, Johannesburg,
an affiliate of
Macmillan Publishing Co. Inc.,
New York

First published 1981

British Library Cataloguing in Publication Data

Escott, John
    The Ghost of Genny Castle. – (Red Lion books; 21)
    1. Readers – 1950-
    I. Title   II. Series
    428.6'2   PE1121

    ISBN 0-304-30702-5

Printed in Hong Kong

Contents

Arrival	5
The Castle Nobody Liked	12
Haunted!	18
The Figure on the Tower	23
The Book in the Attic	30
Breakdown	37
Alexa	42
Footprints	47
The Black Tower	52
Nightmare Fire	55
Afterwards	63

1
Arrival

Walter Burge was working on the roof of his cottage, and he saw the car from his ladder. He had a good view of anything which came along the lane and he recognised the car: Minnie Dawe's.

He watched it as it went round the horseshoe-shaped lane. He could just make out two people sitting in the front. Walter wondered who Minnie Dawe was taking home. A visitor? Walter hoped not.

Visitors were often a nuisance to Walter. There were lots of them in the summer and he hated it. It was a nightmare keeping people away from the castle. But this was winter, and in winter he counted on having a bit of a rest.

He watched the car disappear from sight, then went back to work on the roof of his cottage.

A cat had been sitting at the bottom of the ladder. It got up and padded up the hill towards Genny Castle. It, too, had seen the car.

The lanes twisted between dark trees. Rooks flew up from frozen fields at the noise of the car. They settled on telephone wires.

It was a grey December afternoon. Claire sat in the front of the little car and rubbed her hands together.

Her aunt noticed. 'Cold?' Aunt Min asked.

'A bit,' Claire said. 'Is it much further?'

'About six miles this side of the village,' her aunt said.

They had just come out of the village. It was called Little Genny.

A flutter of snowflakes made patterns on the windscreen. Claire wondered what it was going to be like spending Christmas with her aunt. Aunt Min was her great-aunt really, her mother's aunt.

'It's ten years since I last saw you,' Aunt Min said.

Claire nodded. 'I know,' she said. 'I was only five years old then.'

'And now you're as tall as me,' Aunt Min said. She was small and thin and had wiry grey hair. 'Where is it your mother and father have gone? I have a dreadful memory.'

'New Zealand,' Claire told her. 'Dad's firm sent him out there on business for three months. The three months included Christmas.'

'And your mother's gone with him,' Aunt

Min said.

'Yes,' Claire replied. 'At first she wasn't going. Then the company offered to pay part of her fare and Mum decided she'd like to go. I've been staying at a friend's house during school term.'

'And now you're going to spend Christmas at my little cottage,' Aunt Min said with a smile.

Claire could not remember the cottage any more than she had been able to remember Aunt Min. Her aunt wrote long letters to Claire's mother two or three times a year. She was kind and would make Claire welcome.

Claire had come by train to the nearby town. Her aunt had been at the station to meet her and drive her the rest of the way.

The lane became narrower than ever. Claire stared across the fields, above the hedges. Suddenly, a dark shape appeared in the distance against the grey sky.

'A castle!' Claire said, surprised and pleased.

The tall stone ruin stood high up on a hill. She sat up higher in her seat so that she could see the tall towers. Claire was interested in anything to do with history. In school holidays she often went on trips to see old battlefields, ancient ruins, or museums.

Her bookshelves at home were crammed with guidebooks, postcards and maps.

The lane was in a horseshoe shape. The castle sat in the space at the top of the U. It was a good castle, she decided. You could still see most of the wall and there were three towers, one of which was probably a chapel.

Then she saw the cottage. A small, grey stone building. It sat like a footstool in the field at the bottom of the mound where the castle stood. Smoke curled up from its chimney.

'Is that it?' Claire asked excitedly.

'Is what it?' Aunt Min said. She kept her eyes on the twisting lane, trying to keep the car out of the ditch.

'The cottage at the bottom of the castle,' Claire said. 'Is that yours?'

Aunt Min frowned. 'No, that's not mine. I live further on.' Then she added, 'Well away from that castle.'

It was the way she said it. Her voice dropped almost to a whisper. She seemed nervous.

As the car began to draw level with the castle, Claire saw a figure. It was a man at the top of a ladder. He was working on the roof of the cottage.

'I'll bet he's cold up there,' Claire thought.

Her aunt seemed in a hurry to be home. She didn't look at the castle at all. Claire stared up at the ruin and wondered if it held some sort of secret.

2
The Castle Nobody Liked

The following morning was crisp and clear. Pale sunlight came through the crack between the curtains of Claire's room. Her aunt brought her scrambled eggs and bacon and a cup of tea on a tray.

'Sleep well?' she asked.

'Fine,' Claire told her.

Her aunt drew back the curtains and watched as she ate.

'It's a better morning,' Aunt Min said. 'I have to go to the church to see the vicar. You could come with me and look around the village.'

Claire nodded. 'All right,' she said.

'There's a carol service at the church tomorrow evening,' her aunt explained. 'I play the organ for them.'

'Oh,' Claire said, trying to sound interested.

'You'll be able to come to the service,' Aunt Min said.

'Fine,' she said.

She finished her breakfast.

'I thought I might take a look at the castle,' she said, 'some time while I'm here.'

'The castle?' Again Claire saw the nervous

look on her aunt's face at the mention of the castle.

'I'm interested in castles,' Claire went on.

For a while, her aunt did not speak. Then she said, 'I wouldn't go up there if I were you, Claire. It's not a nice place to visit. It – it isn't – well – safe.'

'How do you mean?' Claire said.

'The building isn't safe,' Aunt Min said. 'It's falling down. There are always bits falling off the walls and towers. And the ground is rough and dangerous.'

She stared out of the window. There was something her aunt wasn't telling her, Claire thought.

An hour later, they were driving into the village. The sun made everything look better. The castle looked beautiful up on the hill. Claire found it difficult to imagine there was anything dangerous about the place. Her aunt saw her looking but did not speak.

'It will be Christmas Eve tomorrow, Claire,' she said when the castle was out of sight.

'Mm? Oh, yes,' Claire said.

Her aunt smiled. 'I was forgetting you are almost sixteen. A little old to be getting excited about Christmas,' she said. 'What about your parents' presents?'

'We did all that before they left,' Claire said. 'They gave me a calculator and some records. And a book about castles,' she added, glancing at her aunt.

'Oh,' Aunt Min said. 'Well I think I'll save my present for you until Christmas Day.'

Claire suddenly realised she had not bought her aunt anything. She had forgotten all about it. She would just have to hope there was somewhere to buy something in Little Genny.

Aunt Min dropped her off near the pub, the Genny Arms. Claire said she would walk up to the church and meet her in an hour.

There was a group of shops and a stone war memorial. Above the rooftops, Claire could see the square tower of the old grey church.

Claire crossed the road and looked in some of the shop windows. She found one shop which seemed to stock almost everything and went inside. There were shelves of groceries at one end. In the centre was a long counter full of magazines and newspapers. At the other end were books, writing paper and envelopes, toys, sweets and tobacco.

The shop was busy at the grocery end. Claire went to look at the books. She had not forgotten that she wanted a present for her aunt. After a while, she decided on a case of writing paper and envelopes. She remembered the long letters her aunt wrote and thought this might be useful.

After she had paid for it, she went back to look at the books.

She wanted something which would tell her about the history of the village and the castle — some sort of guidebook. There were some picture postcards on a stand but none of them was of the castle. Claire thought it was a bit odd. A village was usually proud of its castle if there was one in the area.

'Excuse me,' she said to the woman behind the counter. 'Do you have any books about the castle?'

The woman was tidying newspapers on the counter top and looked up quickly. There were several other women at the counter and they stopped speaking and looked round. Claire saw they were staring at her. She suddenly felt uncomfortable.

'Er — no,' the woman at the counter said. 'We don't.'

She began fiddling with the papers again, not looking at Claire.

'Oh,' Claire said, feeling very awkward. 'Any postcards of it?'

'No,' the woman said shortly.

Claire went back to the bookshelves

and began looking at some paperbacks. She felt silly, as though she had said something wrong. But what? She had only asked about the castle.

It didn't seem to make sense. Nobody seemed to *like* the castle.

3
Haunted!

Claire bought a paperback about old churches. She went outside, feeling the eyes of the women in the shop on her back.

It was a relief to be out in the sunlight again. She pushed the paper-bag with the present for her aunt into her pocket.

A large old car rattled to a halt outside the Genny Arms. Claire watched as a man climbed out. The man wore an old army overcoat which reached down to the top of his heavy boots. He had thick grey hair which touched his shoulders and a short, black pipe in his mouth. He leaned back into the car and took out a shopping bag.

Some women were talking in a group outside the shop. They moved away quickly as the old man approached.

'Always parks on the double yellow line,' a voice said at Claire's side.

She turned to see a boy a few years younger than herself. The boy was nodding towards the car by the kerb. Claire saw that he was right. There were yellow lines by the pavement.

'Doesn't he get pinched for parking there?' Claire asked.

The boy shook his head. 'Not Walter Burge,' he said. 'Nobody has anything to do with Walter Burge. They're afraid of him, if you ask me.'

'Why?' Claire said.

The boy tapped the side of his head. 'He's screwy, see,' he said. 'A bit touched. At least, that's what everybody says. Not surprising. Not when you see where he lives.'

'Where does he live?' Claire asked.

'The cottage in the field at the bottom of the castle,' the boy told her.

'So it was *his* cottage,' Claire said, suddenly interested.

The boy frowned.

'I went past it in my aunt's car,' Claire explained. 'My aunt is Miss Dawe and she lives just outside the village in one of the old farm cottages.'

The boy nodded. 'I know. Are you staying with her for Christmas?'

'That's right,' Claire said. 'But I still don't understand what you were saying. Why would living near the castle drive anybody mad?'

The boy looked around as though worried somebody might be listening. 'It − it's a bad place. Bad things happen there. I've heard my dad talking about it,' he said. He pointed towards the Genny Arms. 'My dad runs the pub.'

'What things have happened at the castle?' Claire asked.

The boy seemed unsure about answering. 'Accidents,' he said at last. 'Some years ago a woman was killed up there. Part of the tallest tower fell down — the Earl's tower it's called. It killed her outright. She was standing underneath.'

'Terrible,' Claire said. 'But accidents happen. It doesn't mean the place is bad because of that.'

'There's more than that,' the boy said. 'Other people have just missed being killed by falling stones and things. And there are great holes in the ground where you least expect them. If you fell down them, heaven knows where you'd end up. Australia, probably.'

Claire laughed. 'Now you're talking daft,' she said.

The boy suddenly looked angry. 'Daft, am I?' he snapped. 'That's what you think. There's — there's *things* happen up there. It's haunted, you know that? Haunted!'

Claire was startled by the look of fear that had suddenly appeared on the boy's face.

'Who is supposed to be haunting it?' she asked.

It was a long time before he answered. '*She* is,' he said at last.

'She?' Claire asked.

'The — the witch,' the boy said quietly.

'Witch!' Claire echoed. She laughed.

The boy looked round quickly. 'Shut up! People around here don't talk about it. And it's nothing to laugh about either.'

Claire stopped laughing. 'But who is this witch supposed to be?' she wanted to know.

At that moment a short, bald-headed man came out of the pub door. 'Alan!' he yelled.

'Here,' the boy shouted back.

'Your mother wants you,' the man said.

'I have to go,' the boy said to Claire, and he moved towards the pub. 'It's true,' he added. 'You want to stay away from that castle!'

4
The Figure on the Tower

Claire walked up the hill towards the church.
It was steep and slippery where the frost had
not melted.

Witches! Claire didn't believe the boy's
story. Funny the way these little country
places always had their old tales. Always a
ghost or something which walked about with
its head under its arm or rattled chains all
over the place. Claire laughed to herself.

She was going to see the castle. She had
made up her mind. No stupid story was
going to put her off. She would not mention
it to her aunt, she decided. Aunt Min would
worry, and she might even try to stop her.

Claire could hear the sound of the organ
coming from the church as she got nearer. It
was playing a carol but she could not
remember the name of it. Her aunt was
obviously practising for the next evening.

She pushed open the heavy door and went
inside. The sound filled the empty church.
There was a tall Christmas tree near the
door, and holly and ivy decorated the walls.

Suddenly a figure appeared from behind
the Christmas tree and Claire jumped.

'Hello,' the figure said.

Claire could see now that it was the vicar. 'Oh – hello,' she said.

'Did I startle you?' the vicar said. He was a fat man with pink cheeks. 'You must be Claire.'

'I am,' Claire said. She was annoyed with herself for being so jumpy.

'Your aunt said you were coming,' the vicar said. 'She tells me you'll be at the service tomorrow evening. Good, good. The more the merrier. It's always popular. Almost everybody comes.'

Claire wondered if 'everybody' included Walter Burge. She decided that it was unlikely. Nobody else would turn up if he did, not if you believed the boy from the pub.

The vicar showed Claire around the church. He told her some of its history. Claire showed him the book she had bought at the shop. There was a bit about the church in it.

'Is it as old as the castle?' Claire asked when they were near the door again.

'Er – no,' the vicar said. 'The – uh – castle is a lot older.'

'I thought so,' Claire said. 'I have a lot of books about castles. I tried to get one about Genny Castle, but they didn't have any in the village shop.'

'No,' the vicar said. 'Um, come and see where the bell-ringers stand. You might hear the bells tomorrow night, after midnight service. The sound carries right outside the village.'

It was clear he did not want to talk about the castle. Another one, Claire thought.

When her aunt had finished playing, she came across.

'Interesting morning, Claire?' she asked.

Claire nodded. 'Quite interesting,' she said.

After lunch, she told her aunt she was going for a walk.

'Don't get lost,' Aunt Min said. 'Stay in the lanes.'

Claire didn't answer. She did not want to say that she would stay in the lanes. She had other plans.

By the time she reached the castle fields, there was an icy wind. The sun was still out but it was much colder than earlier in the day. Even so, it was a nice, bright afternoon, she thought. The sort of afternoon when you laughed about stories of ghosts and witches. The sort of afternoon when you felt brave enough for anything.

She could see the cottage. Walter Burge was back up his ladder. Claire could see him and his car which was parked in the drive by the cottage.

She did not want to be seen so she kept out of sight, stooping near the ground. Then she got to the side of the castle hill and started climbing. It was steep and she had to stop several times to get her breath back.

She moved across the grass and along the dry moat. Now and then she looked down at the stone chimney and the back windows of the cottage. They grew smaller and smaller.

Soon she was up near the dark towers of the castle. The sun was hidden and it was cold. She walked through doorways thick with ivy. It was strangely silent. There was no sound of birds or animals. Everything seemed dead. It was odd.

The cottage was now far below her at the bottom of the steepest part of the hill. Walter Burge was round the other side, safely out of sight.

She went across to the tallest of the towers. There was a doorway at the bottom. Inside, stone steps curled upwards.

Claire shivered. It was as though somebody had put cold arms around her. She wondered if this was the Earl's tower that the boy had mentioned: the one where the woman had died.

She shivered again. There was something

about this place.

'Rubbish!' she said aloud. 'It's stones and grass, nothing else!'

Yet she knew this was not true. There was much more than that. Things had happened here over hundreds of years. Battles and wars, perhaps. They were all part of the stones. As much a part of them as the people who had once lived here. Claire could feel all this inside her, the way she always did when she was in very old places.

Then, as she stepped back from the stairway, she heard a shuffling sound. At first she thought it was a bird swooping away from the top of the tower. She looked up quickly and screamed.

A huge piece of stone was falling away from the top of the tower. It looked like a giant bite from a grey cake. Claire watched it as though it was a slow-motion film, which had nothing to do with her. It bounced twice against the side of the tower and made other, smaller stones fall down in a shower.

Something in her head screamed 'Move!'

She threw herself to one side. The stone hit the ground and split into thousands of pieces. It was so close that she was showered with grey dust. The noise sounded like an explosion.

Claire lay on the grass and stared up at the

top of the tower. Everything seemed fuzzy, but she could not take her eyes from it. She blinked several times. Then her heart seemed to stop.

There was a figure on the top of the tower.

It was a thin, ragged shape with a flame-coloured head. She couldn't see it clearly but it looked like a fire. It hung in mid-air, like a stain against the blue sky; an ugly stain which hovered like a hawk. Claire waited for it to swoop down and attack her.

Then it vanished.

Walter had heard the noise of the stone hitting the ground. He climbed down the ladder and came round the side of his cottage. His face was white. It was as though he knew what had happened without seeing it. He looked up and saw the rising cloud of grey dust.

Then he saw a figure running down the hill.

'Hey!' Walter yelled. 'Hey, you!'

But the figure kept running and Walter knew he would not be able to catch it. The girl – and he was sure it was a girl – would be too fast for his old legs.

He stopped, put his hands on his hips and swore out loud.

5
The Book in the Attic

'Is that you, Claire?' Aunt Min called as she heard the back door close.

'Yes,' Claire answered. She leaned against the door and took a few deep breaths to calm herself.

Her aunt waited for her to come into the living-room. When she did, she was shocked.

'Whatever have you been doing?' Aunt Min said. 'You're covered in grass stains and dust!'

'I – I fell into a ditch.' Claire said the first thing that came into her head. Even now, her heart was thumping away like a washing-machine and she couldn't stop shaking.

'You had better have a bath and change,' her aunt said, looking worried. 'Are you sure you're all right?'

Claire nodded but didn't move. She stood in the doorway and looked around. After a moment, she realised something was different.

'You've put up some Christmas decorations,' she said.

Aunt Min smiled. 'I thought you weren't going to notice,' she said. 'Claire, are you *sure* you're all right?'

'Yes,' Claire said. 'I'll go and have that bath now.'

The hot water relaxed her. What had happened at the castle became like a dream. She began to wonder if she had imagined the whole thing. Especially the figure on the top of the tower. That seemed like part of a nightmare.

It was the shock, she told herself, the shock of nearly being killed. Another inch or two ... She closed her eyes at the thought of it. All sorts of strange things happened when you were suffering from shock, she thought. You saw things which were not really there. You imagined things.

She went down to tea and her aunt watched her carefully as she ate. She did not say anything but Claire wondered if her aunt guessed where she had been.

Later, Claire helped fix some holly behind the pictures and over the doorways. Her aunt really was trying hard to see she enjoyed her stay. Claire was grateful.

'I haven't done this for years,' Aunt Min said. She was as excited as a small child. 'I tried to find the coloured lights I used to have years ago. I think they must be up in the attic. You could go up and have a look in the morning, Claire.'

'All right,' Claire said. She was beginning

to feel more normal now.

She would not go back. Genny Castle could keep its secrets.

The snow came the next day. There was not a great deal at first, just a light covering which brushed everything with white.

Claire went up to the attic to look for the Christmas lights. Her aunt had told her where to look and she found them quite easily.

She was about to take the box down when she spotted a pile of books. If it was going to snow, she thought, she would need something to read that afternoon. She had finished her paperback on old churches the evening before.

She began to look through the pile. Most of the books were novels, the sort her aunt would have enjoyed. Then Claire found a very old book with its cover missing. The pages were yellow with age and it was falling apart. It was only a small, thin book but she saw the title at once: *A History of Genny Castle*.

'Have you found them, Claire?' Her aunt's voice came from downstairs.

'Er – yes,' Claire said. 'Yes, I've found the lights.'

She stuffed the book inside her shirt. For some reason, she didn't want her aunt to know she'd found it.

'Jolly good,' Aunt Min said as Claire came back down. 'We haven't got a Christmas tree but we can hang the lights over the fireplace. They will look nice there.'

The snow had stopped but the sky was still dark. Claire cleared the path outside the cottage and swept the snow off her aunt's old car. They would need it later for the carol service.

Aunt Min spent the afternoon practising carols on her piano. Claire was glad. It gave her a chance to sit and read the book she had found. She kept the paperback about churches at her side, just in case her aunt asked what she was reading.

The book was about the castle's long history. A king and one or two other famous people had stayed in it at different times. All the more reason, Claire thought, for the people of the village to talk about their castle. Only half of the building was left now, she realised as she looked at the maps and drawings.

Halfway through the book Claire found something which made her heart beat faster as she read it. She read the words three times to make sure she had not got it wrong.

They told of a woman who had come to the castle as a servant about two hundred years ago. Nobody seemed to know where she had come from. She just appeared one day. A little while after, things began to happen at the castle. Servants began to fall ill. Animals began to die. It was as though a curse had been placed on the whole castle.

Everyone grew afraid. They began to suspect that there must be some reason for all the misery. Then they discovered herbs and strange medicines in the woman's room.

The new servant woman was a witch, they said. She was making these things happen; it was her fault. While she was alive, nobody would be safe.

Then the fifteen-year-old daughter of the man who owned the castle became ill. It was clear she would die unless something could be done. They told the woman who was a witch to make her well, to use her special powers to cure her.

But the woman would not cure the girl. It was right she should die, the witch said. It was right that the girl's father should suffer. He had had the witch's sister burned some years before. She, too, had been a witch and the man had found this out. It had been at another castle, near London. The servant woman had sworn revenge and now she was going to have it.

A week later, the girl died.

They took the witch to the Earl's tower, right to the very top, where they tied her to a wooden pole and burned her the way her sister had been burned. It was said her screams could be heard six miles away.

According to the book, there had been many stories over the centuries about her haunting the castle. Some said she appeared on the tower. Others, that her screams could still be heard on certain nights and that you could see her long, flame-coloured hair and green eyes.

Claire shut the book quickly. She did not want to know any more.

6
Breakdown

The snow was falling as Claire and her aunt left for the church. The service was to begin at eight o'clock and end at about nine-thirty.

'You can meet me in the church hall afterwards,' her aunt told her. 'We always have cakes and coffee and wish each other Merry Christmas.'

All through the service, Claire was thinking of other things. She sang some of the carols but only half listened to the lessons. She could not forget what she had read. And she could not forget the flame-coloured figure she had seen at the castle.

When it was all over, Claire went across to the church hall. Cakes were laid out on long tables. Women in their best dresses hurried about with cups and saucers.

'Did you enjoy it?' her aunt asked.

'Very much,' Claire told her. She did not want to disappoint her aunt.

She ate and drank while Aunt Min wandered about talking to people. Then she went over to a small window and looked out. Large snowflakes were fluttering down. People were going home. They stepped between the gravestones, trying to find the path. The snow was more than ankle deep.

Claire wondered about their journey back to the cottage. If her aunt didn't stop talking, they would be spending the night at the church hall.

A quarter of an hour later, they left. They stepped outside and the snow fell about them, the icy wind taking their breath away.

'Oh, it's deep, isn't it?' Aunt Min said as snow covered her feet. 'Good job we don't have to do much walking.'

Heads down, they made their way to the car. Claire scraped the frozen snow off the windscreen and back window. Her aunt was having trouble with the door because the lock had frozen. But soon they were inside filling the car with their smoky breath.

The car did not like the weather either. At first it would not start, but then it burst into life and Aunt Min put it into gear.

The tyres made a deep trail in the soft snow on the lane leading away from the church. The windscreen wipers swept to and fro. Claire shivered and peered into the whiteness ahead.

They were at the beginning of the horseshoe-shaped lane when the car began to slide across the road. The tyres had lost their grip in the snow.

'Oh!' Aunt Min cried. She pushed her foot

down on the brake and spun the steering wheel, but it made no difference. The car slid right into the ditch and there was a crunching noise as the front bumper was pulled off by a tree root.

Aunt Min took her shaking hands from the wheel and closed her eyes. 'Oh dear,' she said. 'That's done it.'

She heaved the door open, pushing against the snow. Claire found she could not get the passenger door open because it was right up against a tree trunk. She waited until her aunt had got out, then she slid across the driver's seat.

She sank into the deep snow which had drifted into the ditch. The car was at a crazy angle, its front pointing upwards. The headlights were still on and were lighting the upper branches of the trees.

'We're well and truly stuck,' she said.

'Yes,' Aunt Min agreed. Her voice was still shaking.

Claire walked round to the back of the car. The wheels were buried deep in the snow-filled ditch. The car would have to stay there until it was pulled out by a tractor.

She looked across the fields. In the moonlight, Genny Castle looked frightening. She glanced at her aunt and saw that she too was looking at the castle.

Claire knew what her aunt was thinking. It was a good three miles around the U-shaped lane. Across the fields, it would be less than a mile. But then they would have to pass in front of the castle. They would have to cross Walter Burge's field.

Aunt Min turned and leaned back into the car. She switched off the headlights and took the torch which was under the dashboard. Then she shut the door and locked it.

'We have a walk in front of us, Claire,' she said. 'But we'll take the shortest way, across the fields. I don't think I could manage a three-mile walk around the lane in this wind.'

They found a gate a little way along the lane. It was stuck half-open in the snow.

Claire tried not to look at the castle as she walked. She did not want to see it getting closer.

7
Alexa

Walter Burge was reading a book about the
history of Scottish castles. He was sitting in
the big leather armchair in front of his log
fire. The book lay across his lap.

There were other books in the tiny room,
on shelves, in cupboards and even on the
floor. Walter had collected them over the
years. They were all to do with history.

His cat, Alexa, was curled up beside a pile
of sticks in the fireplace. Her fur was the
same colour as the firelight. Whenever a log
slipped, she would prick up her ears but she
did not move.

Walter was smoking his short, black pipe.
Over the years, smoke from it had stained
the ceiling brown, and sparks had burnt tiny
holes in the furniture.

Walter did not care about such things. All
he cared about was having work to do about
the place, and being near his castle. That
was all he asked of life.

He did not bother with people. He knew
what the village people said about him. They
said he was mad, that he should be left
alone.

And he knew the stories about the castle

being haunted. In fact, he knew more about the castle than any other living person. He did not try to stop the stories. They helped to keep people away. He was glad they were frightened. They *should* be frightened. The castle held its secrets.

The snow settled all around the cottage. The lamp (for there was no electric light) made patterns on the windows. Walter didn't bother with curtains. Nobody ever came to look inside his cottage. His eyes began to close. The book slipped from his lap down into the side of the chair.

Alexa stirred. She stood up in front of the fireplace, stretched, then padded softly out into the passage. She went through to the tiny kitchen at the back. The darkness did not bother her; indeed, she preferred it.

She leapt straight on to the window-sill. Then, with her paw and her nose, undid the window. She pushed it open. She did it easily — she had done it many times before.

Then she dropped softly down into the deep, crisp snow. Shivering only for a moment, she set off, making a trail of footprints up towards Genny Castle.

Some while later, the noise of a log slipping in the flames woke Walter. He stretched his arms above his head.

'Time I was in bed, Alexa,' he muttered.

Then he saw the cat was not there. He pulled himself to his feet and took the oil lamp from the table. The ticking of the grandfather clock in the hall was the only sound in the cottage.

He walked through into the kitchen. 'Alexa?' he said.

Then he noticed the open window and frowned.

'Now why did you have to pick a night like this?' he said with a sigh.

Walter knew where the cat had gone. It was not the first time she had gone to the tower at night. He could remember other nights: nights when strange, wild sounds had been heard coming from the castle; nights when Walter had locked his doors and stayed inside.

Walter tried not to think about these things most of the time. He loved his castle. He did not like the thoughts which crept into the back of his mind.

But the last time there had been trouble.

It had been late, as it usually was. It was a clear night, back in September. He had looked out and seen the orange light of flames against the sky. The top of the Earl's tower seemed to be on fire.

Walter had not been the only one to see it. Some of the people in the village had seen it as well. He heard them talking in the pub and in the village shop. They talked of pulling down the tower if it happened again. The castle was a bad place, they said. If it ever happens again, they said, we'll pull it down. It was an evil building.

He could hear the grandfather clock ticking away the minutes. How long was it since the cat left? How long would it be before ...?

He looked out at the trees and hedges, shining white in the moonlight. And he made up his mind. He would fetch Alexa back. He would have to. Something terrible might happen.

Walter went back into the living-room. He pulled on his boots, his heavy overcoat, and the woolly hat which he had knitted himself. Then he took a storm lamp from the cupboard and left the other, larger lamp burning on the table.

Then Walter went out into the wintry night.

8
Footprints

Claire had snow in her shoes and her face was so cold she could not feel any part of it. Even her eyelids seemed frozen over.

And she was worried about her aunt. Aunt Min was too old to be out in this weather. Every so often she would stop and shiver, and when Claire saw her face in the light of the moon she was shocked. It was bluey-white and wet with tears. The old woman's skin seemed to be stretched tightly across her cheekbones and her breath came in short gasps.

It had been a difficult walk. The snow was deep and clung to their legs like invisible hands. Claire decided that her aunt would not be able to manage the rest of the distance. They would have to find shelter. Aunt Min would have to rest.

Claire looked at the cottage ahead. It was quite near. The front door was shut, like a black hand held up to them. But there was nowhere else.

'The cottage,' she shouted above the noise of the wind. 'We'll stop there for a bit.'

At first Aunt Min did not seem to understand what Claire was saying. Then a

look of horror crept over her face. She began
to shake her head. Then she almost fell.

'The cottage,' Claire said firmly. 'We have
to go there.'

They struggled to the front door. Her aunt
was shaking and Claire held her arm tightly.
She banged on the door but there was no
answer.

'Round the back,' Claire shouted. And she
half carried Aunt Min round the side of the
cottage.

They both saw Walter's footprints leading
up to the castle.

Even so, Claire thumped at the back door.
Then she turned the handle and found she
was able to push it open. Aunt Min tried to
say something but she was too short of
breath.

The warmth from the cottage was
welcoming and they could see the light down
the passage.

Claire led her aunt to the chair where
Walter had been sitting. Aunt Min sank into
it. Then Claire went and stood by the fire.
After a moment, her fingers and ears began
to hurt from the sudden heat and she had to
move away.

Her aunt needed some sort of hot drink,
she thought. She looked round the room. An
old, blackened kettle stood in the fireplace.

Beside it was a teapot and a flowered mug with the remains of some tea in the bottom.

Claire used some water from the kettle to swill out the cup. She threw the dregs on to the fire and it hissed back like a startled cat. Then she put the kettle on the log fire and looked into the teapot. Tea leaves were stuck to the bottom. There was no sign of milk or sugar, but she hoped her aunt would not mind.

She looked at her watch and was shocked to see the time: eleven o'clock. The walk had taken longer than she thought; much longer.

Aunt Min's eyes were closed and her face was grey with tiredness. Claire would not be able to take her any further on foot.

After she had made the mug of tea, Claire woke her aunt.

'Something hot to drink,' she told her.

'Oh – thank you,' Aunt Min said. 'I feel a little better now.'

'You can't walk any more tonight,' Claire said.

'No,' Aunt Min agreed. 'I don't think I can.'

'I'll go and find Mr Burge,' Claire said. 'Maybe he could take us back in his car.'

Aunt Min looked frightened. 'Where is he?' she asked.

'I think he's up at the castle,' Claire said.

'I'll have to go and find him.'

'Claire,' her aunt began. She could hardly find enough strength to talk. 'You can't. The castle ...'

'I know about the castle,' Claire said quietly. 'It doesn't matter. I'm not afraid.'

It wasn't true. She was afraid, very afraid. But she took the torch from her aunt and left the old woman sipping the hot, black tea.

9
The Black Tower

Walter Burge struggled against the strong wind. His face stung and every so often he could feel a pain in his chest which made him stop. He was too old for this, he told himself.

'Alexa!' he called. But the word was carried away by the wind.

He kept looking up at the tower. It was black against the sky. He thought he saw a glow, but then it vanished. He had not seen it, he told himself.

He was afraid and he knew it. He had never been up to the castle at night. He had never followed Alexa on her trips into the darkness. He did not want to see or know what happened.

Now he had to face it. Things *did* happen. Alexa was no ordinary cat. Alexa was — *somebody else*.

'Alexa,' he said to himself.

It had been the name of the woman servant, the one who had been burned. He had read the story when he was a boy, when his father and mother had lived at the cottage and farmed the fields around it. He had always known about Alexa the servant woman.

Alexa with the flame-coloured hair.

Then, ten years ago, the cat had turned up on his doorstep. He had thought it was a stray. He even shooed it away to begin with. But it kept coming back and it kept going up to the castle.

He had called the cat Alexa because of the colour of its fur. Once he thought that was funny. He didn't any more.

A year later, things began to happen. A cow from a nearby farm got into the castle grounds. It was found dead the next day. No reason could be found.

Then the same thing happened to a dog from the village. It was found dead in the dry moat of the castle.

Then a woman had been killed. She had been found dead at the bottom of the Earl's tower. A heavy stone had crushed her head.

Two other people had slipped over and broken bones.

A child was trapped in a dungeon and almost died. He had not spoken a word since.

Then people began to see lights and things moving up among the towers but when they went to look, there was nothing there.

Once there had been rabbits and small animals living around the castle. Birds had nested among the stones. Suddenly they all vanished. Now and then the remains of a dead bird could be found, but that was all.

People stayed away. Walter was the only one who would go up to the castle and then only by day.

Until now.

'Alexa!' he called again.

But there was silence except for the noise of the wind.

She sat on the tower. She saw the old man with the lamp swinging in his hand. Then, further away, she noticed a smaller figure.

It was the girl. The girl who had come before. There was something about the girl that frightened her. It was as if she had come for a special reason. This was the feeling Alexa had, and she always took notice of her feelings.

Her green eyes became narrow and her orange fur began to glow. Gradually, the glow grew larger, like a fire.

The girl had escaped last time. She must not escape again.

10
Nightmare Fire

The effort of the climb made Claire forget
about being afraid. Once or twice she
thought she saw the light of a lamp up
ahead. But it could have been a star, or the
moonlight on the snow.

She followed the footmarks and soon
realised where they were leading. Walter
Burge had gone up to the tower. But why?
And with what? She could see what looked
like paw-marks of a cat beside the footmarks.

Claire wondered if Walter was mad. Did
he climb the tower every night at midnight
for some special reason?

She reached the doorway of the Earl's
tower. She had to choose. She could climb
up, or wait until the old man came down. It
was no good shouting to him. Walter would
never hear her voice against the noise of the
wind.

She thought of her aunt's tired, grey face.
She should be home in bed, and as soon as
possible.

Claire stepped into the tower and started to
climb up the wet, slippery stones of the
staircase. Moonlight shone through the
window slits, and with it came a blast of

wind. It almost pushed her off the stairs. There was no handrail, only cracks in the wall to hold on to.

After a while, she knew she must be near the top. She seemed to have been climbing for hours. Her legs hurt and her feet weighed a ton.

And then she saw the light up ahead.

It was bright orange. Suddenly, there was a low moan. At first Claire thought it was the sound of the wind, but then the noise grew louder and she knew that it wasn't.

She froze on the spot.

Then there was another noise: a crackling, spitting noise. Claire realised what it was. *It was the sound of a fire burning.*

She would have to go back down. Now! But her feet wouldn't move!

Where was Walter Burge? He must be up there. His footprints had led into the tower. There had been no footprints coming out again.

He might need help, Claire thought. She forced herself to climb on.

'Mr Burge!' she shouted. 'Mr Burge!'

Walter was in the middle of a great orange light. He could not see through it. It seemed to be sucking him into its centre. There were

flames but he could feel nothing — no pain. His eyes hurt from the light, but that was all.

He could hear the noise which was now growing into a high shriek. It seemed to fill the whole night. His head rang with the sound of her screams.

'Alexa!' he shouted. 'Alexa! Stop! Stop this!'

Faintly, in the background, he could hear something else. What was it? A voice?

'Mr Burge ... Mr Burge.'

'Who is it?' he called. 'What's happening?'

'It's Claire,' the voice said faintly.

'Claire? I don't know any Claire,' he said. He felt dizzy. He felt as though he was being swept away by a great river. Hands seemed to be all around him, pulling him away.

Claire? Claire? *Claire?*

He *did* know a Claire! Now who − ?

And then he remembered. She had been the girl who died. The daughter of the man who owned the castle. *Her* name had been Claire. He could remember reading it in several of the books he had about Genny Castle.

'Claire?' he said. 'You're Claire? But Claire is dead.'

Something else was saying the name now. He could hear it. It was a whispering sound and seemed to be part of the flames.

'*Claire ... Claire ... Claire?*'

It sounded shocked.

'*Not dead? ... Alive? ... Alive?*'

Suddenly the light began to fade. Walter Burge could see the sky above him and the tower around him now.

'*Not dead? ... Claire? ... Alive?*'

The whispering was growing fainter. It was as though a fire was being put out.

Soon all that was left was the faint light of the lamp in Walter's hand.

Claire climbed up the last few steps and out on to the top of the tower. The icy wind swept around her, making her eyes water.

Walter Burge was standing at the edge of the tower. He was looking across the snowy fields. Yet although his eyes stared, Claire realised he was not seeing what was around him.

On the wall of the tower stood the flame-coloured cat. She looked straight at Claire and her bright eyes seemed afraid. She shrank away at the sight of the girl, as though Claire was a ghost.

Walter noticed the light from Claire's torch. He turned quickly, and leant against the wall, half afraid.

In the pale light, Claire saw a crack appear in the stones. The wall moved slightly as Walter put his weight against it.

'Look out!' Claire shouted.

The voice didn't sound like her own, yet it was. And it was real enough to make Walter jump away from the wall as if he had been bitten. He dropped the lamp. The glass smashed and the light went out.

The crumbling stones behind Walter tumbled into the black space below. Half of one side of the tower slipped away. A cloud of snow and dust rose upwards.

Claire and Walter ran for the stairs.

When the noise stopped and the dust had settled, the two of them looked back at what was left of the top of the tower.

'Heaven help us, girl,' breathed Walter. 'That was a close one!'

'Your cat,' Claire whispered. 'What happened to your cat?'

They found the body when they reached the ground. The limp body with the flame-coloured fur lay twisted and broken in the snow.

'It's for the best,' Walter said to himself, staring at the cat.

Claire did not ask what he meant. She did not want to know the answer.

11
Afterwards

Aunt Min had fallen asleep. She woke with a start at the sound of footsteps in the passage.

Walter Burge came in, followed by Claire.

'M – Mr Burge,' Aunt Min began. 'I – we ...'

'The girl's explained,' Walter said.

'Oh,' she said. She looked at Claire. 'Is everything all right?'

Claire nodded without speaking.

'Had a bit of a shock,' Walter said. He nodded towards the castle. 'Part of the tower fell down. I expect it was the weight of the snow.'

Aunt Min looked from one to the other. 'I see,' she said.

'I'll take you home in my car,' Walter said. 'I'll take a rope and pull yours out of the ditch tomorrow.'

'Oh, thank you, Mr Burge,' Aunt Min said.

They went outside to Walter's car. It had stopped snowing and the wind had dropped a little. Suddenly they heard the bells of the village church. It was the end of the midnight service.

Claire looked at her watch. 'It's Christmas

Day,' she said. She had completely forgotten the time.

They sat in the back of Walter's old car. Her aunt stared at the back of Walter's head. Claire looked out of the back window, up towards the castle ruin.

It seemed different from down here. It did not look so evil. The shape of the Earl's tower had changed. It was not as tall any more.

'Good job you were with me tonight, Claire,' Aunt Min said. 'I don't know what would have happened if I'd been coming back from the carol service on my own.'

Claire wondered what might have happened if she had not arrived at the top of the Earl's tower when she did. Walter glanced back and she knew he was thinking the same thing.

When Walter went up to the castle the next morning, the body of the flame-coloured cat had gone. Walter had come to bury her but the place where she had fallen was empty.

It was as though she had never been.